Rabbits

Heather Hammonds

Contents

Pet Rabbits

Rabbits are small animals that can be kept as pets.

Lots of people keep pet rabbits at home.
Some schools keep pet rabbits, too.

There are white rabbits
and black rabbits.
There are brown rabbits
and grey rabbits.

There are rabbits with spots, too!

Looking After Rabbits

Rabbits can be kept
in a **hutch**.

The hutch can be put inside a house
or out in the garden.

Rabbits sleep, eat and play
in their hutch.

There are white rabbits
and black rabbits.
There are brown rabbits
and grey rabbits.

There are rabbits with spots, too!

Rabbits have long ears.
They move their ears around
to help them hear things.

Rabbits have whiskers on their nose,
and sharp teeth inside their mouth.

Rabbits have four legs
and a little tail.
They can hop around very quickly.

Some rabbits are small.
Other rabbits are very big.

Looking After Rabbits

Rabbits can be kept
in a **hutch**.

The hutch can be put inside a house
or out in the garden.

Rabbits sleep, eat and play
in their hutch.

Rabbits need lots of clean straw
in their hutch.

They need lots of room to hop around,
and toys to play with, too.

A rabbit hutch needs to be out of the sun
on hot days, so the rabbits can stay cool.

Rabbits need lots of water to drink
and the right food to eat.

They must have clean water and food
every day.

Rabbits need to eat lots of **hay**
and some green vegetables.
They can eat fruit sometimes, too.

Other vegetables are not good for rabbits
and they must not eat them.

Rabbits need to eat more of these foods.

Rabbits can sometimes eat these foods.

These foods are not good for rabbits.

Baby Rabbits

Baby rabbits are called **kits**, or kittens.
A mother rabbit will make a nest
with some of her fur.
She will have her kits in the warm nest.

At first, kits have no fur.
They cannot open their eyes.
Their ears are shut, too!

The kits drink milk from their mother.

Little kits quickly get bigger.
Their eyes and ears open,
and they soon have fur.

The kits come out of their nest
and begin to play together.
They start to eat hay and other rabbit food.

What Rabbits Do

Rabbits like to come out of the hutch and run, hop and jump around.

They can play in toy tunnels or dig a hole.

Rabbits like to play with toys that they can eat, too.

This toy has hay inside of it for the rabbit to eat.

It is fun to play with pet rabbits and look after them.

Glossary

hay long, dry grass

hutch a home to keep small animals in

kits baby rabbits